√98

LARGE PRINT  WITHDRAWN FELDHEYM

Garlock, Dorothy

Wild sweet wilderness
c1995

14√8/02
31√2/14
33√ 10/18

M

Wild Sweet Wilderness

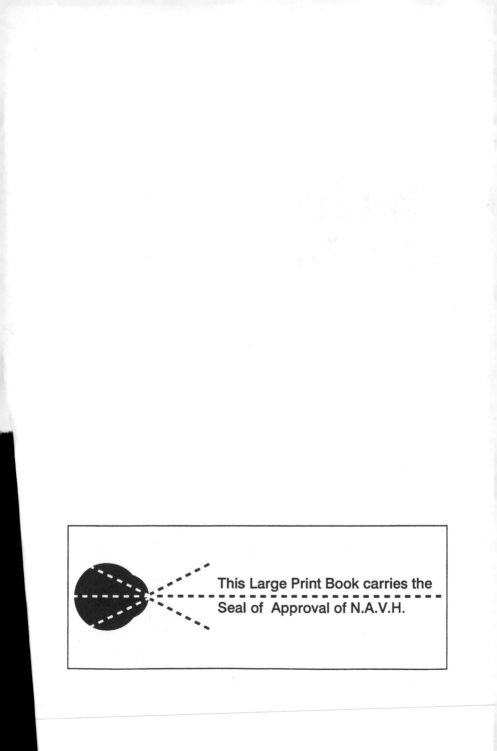

This Large Print Book carries the
Seal of Approval of N.A.V.H.